PUFFIN BOOKS

BAD BECKY IN TROUBLE

Gervase Phinn is a teacher, freelance lecturer, author, poet, educational consultant, school inspector, visiting professor of education and last, but by no means least, father of four. Most of his time is spent in schools with teachers and children. Gervase lives in Doncaster with his family.

D1321543

GERVASE PHINN

Bad Becky in Trouble

Illustrated by Lindsey Gardiner

PUFFIN

PUFFIN BOOKS

Published by the Penguin Group
Penguin Books Ltd, 80 Strand, London WC2R 0RL, England
Penguin Group (USA) Inc., 375 Hudson Street, New York, New York 10014, USA
Penguin Group (Canada), 10 Alcorn Avenue, Toronto, Ontario, Canada M4V 3B2
(a division of Pearson Penguin Canada Inc.)
Penguin Ireland, 25 St Stephen's Green, Dublin 2, Ireland (a division of Penguin Books Ltd)
Penguin Group (Australia), 250 Camberwell Road, Camberwell, Victoria 3124, Australia
(a division of Pearson Australia Group Pty Ltd)
Penguin Books India Pvt Ltd, 11 Community Centre, Panchsheel Park, New Delhi – 110 017, India
Penguin Group (NZ), cnr Airborne and Rosedale Roads, Albany, Auckland 1310, New Zealand
(a division of Pearson New Zealand Ltd)
Penguin Books (South Africa) (Pty) Ltd, 24 Sturdee Avenue, Rosebank, Johannesburg 2196, South Africa

Penguin Books Ltd, Registered Offices: 80 Strand, London WC2R 0RL, England

www.penguin.com

First published 2005
1

Text copyright © Gervase Phinn, 2005
Illustrations copyright © Lindsey Gardiner, 2005
All rights reserved

The moral right of the author and illustrator has been asserted

Set in Perpetua

Made and printed in England by Clays Ltd, St Ives plc

British Library Cataloguing in Publication Data
A CIP catalogue record for this book is available from the British Library

ISBN 0–141–31808–2

For my daughter, Elizabeth

Contents

Becky Goes Fishing

'Well, I want to go!'
shrieked Becky,
stamping her foot
so hard on the hall
carpet that little
puffs of dust rose
into the air. Dad and
her two brothers,
Bernard and Ben, were
going fishing and
they were not taking
her with them. She thought it was very,
very unfair. 'I want to! I want to! I want
to go fishing!'

Becky's twin brothers scowled at her. The thought of their impossible little sister tagging along on their fishing trip filled them with dread. Taking Becky would mean only one thing – trouble.

'Fishing is for boys,' said Bernard firmly.

'Girls play with dolls; they don't fish,' added Ben.

'I don't want to play with soppy old dolls,' Becky told them, sticking out her tongue and pulling the most awful face. 'I want to go fishing.'

Becky liked playing football, climbing up trees, looking for creepy-crawlies in the garden, walking along the tops of walls, having water fights and stomping in the mud. She definitely did not like sitting in her room with a doll on her knee.

'Well, you are not coming!' shouted Bernard.

'There's no way!' agreed Ben.

'I am!' Becky yelled back, thumping her hands on her hips. 'I am! I am! I am!'

'What is all this noise about?' asked Dad, coming into the hall.

'I want to go fishing with you and the twins,' Becky told him, frowning.

'Don't let her, Dad,' begged Bernard. 'She'll spoil it. She always does.'

'She'll throw stones in the water and frighten all the fish away,' added Ben angrily.

'I won't,' said Becky. 'I'll be really, really good.'

'Huh!' cried Ben. 'You are *never* really, really good.'

'You wouldn't know how to be good,' added Bernard.

'Wouldn't you rather stay at home,' said Dad, putting his arm round Becky's shoulders, 'and help Mum bake that big chocolate cake for tomorrow's tea?'

'No, I wouldn't,' said Becky, sticking out her bottom lip. 'I don't like soppy baking. I want to go fishing.'

'Or you could go into town with Mum,' coaxed Dad. 'She's going shopping and she might buy you a pretty new dress. You'd like that, wouldn't you?'

'No, I would not! I hate shopping and I hate pretty dresses!' Becky exclaimed. She much preferred wearing jeans and trainers. 'I told you, I want to go fishing. It's not fair that you're taking the twins and leaving me at home.'

Becky then thought of something very clever to say. She looked up at Dad with a glimmer of mischief in her eyes and said quietly, 'I could get up to all sorts of trouble at home while Mum's cooking and if I go into town I might get lost . . .'

Dad sighed. He knew when he was beaten. 'Oh, very well,' he said, 'but you have to be very, very good.'

'Yes! Yes! Yes!' Becky punched the air and jumped up and down, causing puffs of dust to rise up out of the carpet for the second time that morning. 'I'm going fishing!'

'Oh no,' moaned Bernard.

'Oh, Dad,' groaned Ben.

Becky sat on the back seat, sandwiched between her two scowling brothers.

It was a hot day and the sun shone brightly in a clear blue sky. Dad and the twins were wearing T-shirts and shorts. Becky, on the other hand, was wrapped up like an Arctic explorer. She had on her bright-yellow anorak with the fur-edged hood, her thick orange jumper, some old jeans, her long green scarf with matching gloves and a pair of big

black rubber boots. This was exactly
what Becky had seen fishermen on the
television wearing and she wanted to be
just like them.

'You will be
far too hot
and sticky in
all that,' Dad
warned.
'No, I
won't,'
replied
Becky
stubbornly.
'But it's a
lovely bright
sunny day,' he

told her. 'Why don't you go and put on a nice cool sundress and some sandals instead?'

'Eeeek!' squealed Becky. 'I hate sundresses and I hate sandals.'

'Can we get going, please?' pleaded Bernard.

'The fish will have all been caught by the time we get there,' grumbled Ben.

'Oh, very well,' said Dad, and started the car.

At the riverbank, Becky stood and stared at the rippling water to see if she could see any fish. Bernard got out the rods, Ben sorted out the fishing lines with hooks and Dad opened a big round metal tin. Inside were hundreds of wriggling maggots.

'Uuuurrrgghh!' cried Bernard, shuddering in disgust.

'Uuuurrrrgghh!' squealed Ben, backing away.

'Don't worry,' said Dad, smiling. 'I'll put them on your hooks.'

'I like maggots,' said Becky, coming over and picking up a few of the white wriggling creatures and cupping them in her hands. 'They're cute and they tickle. I'm not going to put them on my hook. I'm going to use a big fat squiggly squelchy worm instead.'

'But fish like maggots,' Bernard told her.

'They don't like worms,' said Ben.

– 'Well, I'm using a worm,' Becky informed them. 'I can if I want.'

'Very well,' said Dad, shaking his head and smiling, 'but you'll not catch anything.'

We'll see about that, Becky thought to herself.

While Dad and the twins cast in their lines, Becky dug with a stick in the soft earth by the riverbank until she found a long pink worm. She put it on her hook, made herself comfortable at the edge of the river and dangled her fishing line into the water.

'Not there, Becky,' said Dad. 'It's much too bright in the middle of the river. Fish like it in the shade, where it's dark and cool, under the branches of the trees.'

'Well, I like it here,' said Becky obstinately, staying exactly where she was.

'Very well,' sighed Dad. 'But as I said, you won't catch anything like that.'

They all sat in silence for a while, concentrating on their lines and looking for a tremble on the rod that would tell them there was a fish on the end of the hook. But then the weather suddenly changed. The sun disappeared behind a large dark cloud and lost all of its heat and the river became quite choppy.

'Brrrrr,' said Dad, rubbing his arms.

'It's freezing,' said Bernard, shivering.

'I wish I'd brought a coat,' said Ben.

Becky felt as snug as a bug in a rug in her anorak, jeans, thick jumper, scarf and gloves. 'I'm lovely and warm,' she told everyone smugly.

Her brothers pulled gruesome faces. Dad smiled to himself.

Just then Becky's line gave a jerk.

'Oh!' she exclaimed in surprise. She pulled on her rod and it bent. She tugged and heaved and the rod bent some more. There was something heavy on the end of her line.

'I've caught a fish!' she cried. 'I've caught a fish!'

'Looks like a whopper,' shouted Dad, forgetting about being cold and running along the riverbank to where Becky was sitting. 'Here, let me land it for you.'

'I want to land it myself,' Becky told him with a determined look on her face.

'You're not strong enough,' said Bernard. 'You'll lose it.'

'You're pulling too hard,' said Ben. 'You'll snap the line.'

But Becky ignored their advice and she tugged and heaved some more until

suddenly the rod flew towards her and
out of the river came a big black boot
dangling on the end of her line. It was
dripping with muddy
water and full of slimy
green weeds.

'It's a boot,'
chortled Bernard,
stabbing the air with
his finger.

'She's caught a
boot,' cackled Ben.

The twins put down their rods and
ran up and down the bank chanting,
'Becky's caught a boot! Becky's caught a
boot!'

Becky scowled at them.

'Take no notice, Becky,' said Dad, winking. 'It's more than your brothers have caught.'

They settled themselves back down by the riverbank and waited for the fish to bite. Becky stayed perfectly still and watched her line like a hungry cat watching a tank of goldfish. She didn't move a muscle. She was determined to catch a big fat fish this time. Her dad had never seen her so quiet before and decided that he would definitely bring her along again.

After a while the weather got worse. The wind picked up and it began to spit with rain.

'I think we had better call it a day,' said Dad, looking up gloomily at the dark clouds in the sky.

'Yes,' agreed Bernard, stamping his feet against the cold.

'We've not had a bite all morning,' said Ben, blowing on his hands to warm them up.

'Shall we go, then?' asked Dad.

'No!' cried Becky, crossing her arms defiantly. 'I like it here. Fishing's fun. I'm staying.' And, just then, there was a sudden jerk on her rod and the line went taut. Becky jumped to her feet and tugged and heaved. There was something heavy on the end of her line. 'I've caught something!' she cried.

'Probably another boot,' laughed Bernard.

'Now you'll have a matching pair,' sniggered Ben.

Becky gripped the rod tightly and pulled with all her might. The rod curved and quivered and then bent so much it looked as if it would snap in two. But Becky gave one mighty heave and out of the river leapt a great silver fish. It splashed and thrashed on the top of the water.

'It *is* a fish!' cried Dad in surprise. 'It's a whopper! Here, Becky, let me help you.'

'I'm going to land it myself,' Becky declared, puffing and panting as the fish pulled on the line.

'You're too small,' said Bernard. 'You'll lose it.'

'You're pulling too hard,' said Ben, just like the last time. 'You'll snap the line.'

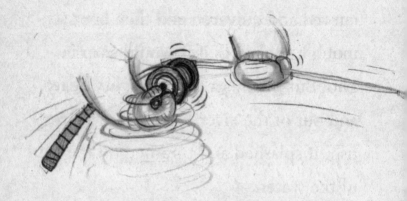

But Becky carried on reeling it in, all the time watching the great silver fish leaping and splashing in the murky water.

'Well done!' said Dad. 'It looks like fish for supper tonight.'

The fish was close to the bank now and Becky was feeling very pleased with herself. She looked at the fish twisting and thrashing on the end of the line and thought about Mum's startled expression when Becky appeared at the door holding her catch. She would probably take a photograph and Becky could take it to school to show her teacher, Miss Drear.

When Becky had reeled in all of the line, Dad unhooked the fish and held it out to Becky. 'What a catch,' he said.

'Wow!' exclaimed the twins.

The fish writhed in Dad's hand,
gasping for air. Becky looked at it
carefully. It was beautiful — with shiny
silver scales, small button eyes, delicate
pale-green fins and a great curve of tail.

Becky made a sudden decision.

'I'm putting him back in the river,' she told Dad.

'Putting it back!' cried the twins together.

'He's my fish,' Becky told them. 'I caught him and I can do what I want with him, can't I, Dad?'

'You certainly can,' Dad reluctantly agreed. He had been looking forward to fish with parsley sauce for supper. But he smiled and gently placed the great silver creature in Becky's hands. 'Hold him tightly; he's very slippery.'

Becky held the cold slimy body firmly. She felt the fish panting and saw its gills moving in and out. She bent down and placed it carefully in the water. It stayed still for a moment just beneath the surface and then, with a great swish of its tail, it was gone, deep, deep down into the murky depths.

A few bubbles came to the surface.

'He was saying thank you,' said Becky. She felt really pleased that she had let it go and not taken it home. After all, she thought, they could go to the fish and chip shop any time.

The huge drops of rain that had been steadily plopping on to the water started hammering down now. Within seconds of the heavens opening, Dad and the twins were soaked to the skin and shivering with cold.

Becky put up her hood. She was nice and warm, and dry as a bone.

There was a mad scramble as Dad and the twins packed up the fishing gear and headed towards the car. Down the riverbank they ran, squelching in the mud and clutching their rods and fishing tackle, with Becky calmly following behind.

Just as they were about to reach the car, Dad leapt over the stump of a dead tree and lost his footing. 'Aaaaah!' he cried and fell on his face with a SPLAT!

Then Bernard's sandals slipped in the mud and his legs shot from under him, causing him to land on his bottom with a thump. Ben, who didn't have time to slow down, tumbled over his brother and slithered in the mud next to him.

Becky smiled and then she giggled and then she laughed until the tears rolled down her cheeks. She had never seen

anything quite as funny as Dad and the twins in a big muddy heap on the ground. She was very glad she had put her boots on.

Mum laid big sheets of newspaper on the kitchen floor before they were allowed into the house.

'Just look at the state of you!' she said, shaking her head at the twins and Dad. Then she caught sight of Becky, smirking. 'Well, at least someone has managed to stay clean.'

Dad looked grumpy. The twins glowered.

'Did you all have a nice time?' Mum asked them.

'Dreadful,' grumbled Dad.

'Awful!' moaned Bernard.

'Terrible,' groaned Ben.

'Fantastic!' cried Becky. 'Can we go again next Saturday, Dad?'

Becky and the School Inspector

At a quarter past eight each morning, Bernard and Ben would leave home with Becky and take her to school – out of the gate, down the street, through the park, across the busy main road and up the little path that led to the school gates.

Becky knew her way to school perfectly well and hated being escorted by her brothers, especially having to hold both their hands when they got to the main road. However, no matter how many times she complained, Mum and Dad would not take no for an answer. And for once, Becky knew it was no use arguing with them.

One bright autumn morning, the three of them, as usual, were walking through the park on their way to school. Becky loved this time of year. She liked to run through the piles of dead leaves and kick them in the air. She liked jumping on the acorns that littered the ground, crunching them noisily under her feet. And she loved searching for conkers to throw in the duck pond. Of course, that was only if the park keeper wasn't around.

On this particular morning, as she was looking around for the next pile of leaves to run through, Becky noticed a man with a very wrinkly face approaching them. He had snow-white hair, small green eyes, a sharp nose, large red ears and a narrow slit of a mouth. He wore a long raincoat and carried a big black bag and stood in front of them in the middle of the path.

'Excuse me,' said the man pleasantly, when the children came to a standstill, 'I wonder if one of you young people could tell me where Parksview School is?'

That's my school, thought Becky staring up at the towering figure.

The tall man smiled. 'I seem to have got myself a little lost. The school must be somewhere near here.'

Before either of the twins could answer, Becky snapped, 'No!'

'I beg your pardon?' said the man looking very surprised.

'No,' repeated Becky. 'We can't tell you. Go away!'

The tall man peered down at Becky. He tried again. 'I am looking for Parksview School and wondered if one of you children –'

'If you don't go away,' warned Becky, placing her hand firmly on her hips and giving him her most horrid stare (the one which could turn milk sour and freeze soup in pans), 'I'll scream and scream.'

'Becky!' said Ben. 'Don't be so rude.'

'It's just over —' began Bernard.

'Mum and Dad have told us not to talk to strangers in parks,' interrupted his sister.

'What?' exclaimed the man.

'We're not supposed to speak to strangers,' repeated Becky. 'So go away! Clear off!'

'B-b-b-but —' stuttered the man.

'Go away or I'll kick you, really really hard.' Becky was getting impatient and wanted to get to school.

'You are a very, very rude little girl,' said the man angrily, glowering at her. 'What is your name?'

'Mary Poppins. What's yours?' replied Becky, sticking out her tongue. Before the man could answer she skipped off, kicking leaves in every direction and crunching acorns. 'Come on,' she shouted to her brothers, 'or we'll be late.'

The twins shrugged and followed their sister, knowing it was pointless arguing with Becky when she was in one of her determined moods. They left the man on the path standing with his small mouth open, staring after them.

'You shouldn't speak like that to adults,' said Bernard when he had caught up with his sister.

'We've been told not to talk to strangers,' said Becky. 'He might have wanted to kidnap me.'

'Huh!' snorted Ben. 'Kidnap you? If he did, he'd soon be paying Mum and Dad to take you back.'

There was something different about grumpy Mrs Groucher, the head teacher, that morning. For a start, instead of wearing her old baggy brown skirt and lumpy cardigan, she had on a new bright flowery dress.

And, instead of glaring at the children and shouting at them to be quiet as they filed into assembly, as she usually did, the head teacher had a silly smile on her face and was acting very strangely.

'Good morning, children,' she trilled. 'What a lovely day. How smart and well-behaved you all are.' Even when she caught sight of Becky stomping into the hall, her pockets bulging with conkers, Mrs Groucher didn't stop smiling. 'Rebecca, dear,' she said, 'why don't you come and sit down at the front?'

'I want to sit at the back, Mrs Groucher,' said Becky.

'Well, I would like you to sit at the front, dear.' Mrs Groucher's voice sounded just the tiniest bit sharp. 'Down here, Rebecca, please, where I can see you.'

'Oh, phooey!' grumbled Becky under her breath.

As she stamped her way down to the front of the hall, the conkers in her pockets spilled out and bounced across the floor. The other children scurried to pick them up.

'They're mine!' cried Becky.

'My goodness,' said the head teacher, 'what a lot of conkers you have, Rebecca. Just leave them there and you

can have them back at morning break.'
Becky paused, waiting for the head
teacher to begin her usual shouting,
finger pointing and telling off, but it
didn't happen. 'Come along, Rebecca,
dear,' she said, smiling instead.

*There is something very odd about grumpy
Mrs Groucher this morning*, Becky thought
to herself.

Then, as she plonked herself between
Simon and Araminta in the front row, she
caught sight of him. Until now he had
been hidden behind the
piano. There he sat,
with his wrinkled face,
snow-white hair, small
green eyes, sharp nose,

large red ears and narrow slit of a mouth. Next to him was the big black bag. It was the stranger who had stopped them earlier that morning in the park.

'We have a visitor, today, children,' chirped Mrs Groucher. 'A very, very important visitor.' She beamed in the direction of the strange man. 'This is Mr Scruple and he's a school inspector. He's come to see all the lovely, lovely work you are doing. The children here, Mr Scruple,' said Mrs Groucher, in a sing-song sort of voice, 'are extremely well behaved, hard-working and polite.'

'Really?' said the school inspector, staring hard at Becky.

She pulled her most horrid face. If he

thought he was going to make her shiver
with fear and go red with embarrassment,
he was wrong.

'Mrs Groucher,' Becky called out,
waving her hand in the air like a daffodil
in a strong wind.

'Yes, dear?' said Mrs Groucher, her
silly, silly smile becoming slightly
strained.

'Mrs Groucher,' asked Becky, 'we're not supposed to talk to strangers on our way to school, are we?'

'Certainly not!' exclaimed the head teacher. 'If anyone approaches you, anyone at all who you do not know, you must not, under any circumstances, talk to them.'

'I thought so,' said Becky, smiling wickedly.

'Police Constable Catchum came into school last week,' Mrs Groucher informed Mr Scruple proudly, 'and told the children never to talk to strangers.' The school inspector went a deep shade of red. Becky grinned.

*

Later that morning Mr Scruple arrived at
Miss Drear's classroom. He turned a
shade paler when he caught sight of Becky
splashing paint on a big piece of paper.
She had red paint on her hands, yellow

paint on her face and green paint on her dress. She was having a marvellously messy time. Becky loved painting. Her pictures were bold and colourful and usually featured man-eating monsters, many-headed aliens, bloodthirsty pirates and killer sharks.

The school inspector moved as far away from her as he could.

'What delightful work,' he said to Araminta, as he flicked though the pages of her writing book. 'It is so neat and tidy.'

'I like writing,' Araminta told him sweetly. 'That's my story about the beautiful Princess Charisma and the handsome prince.'

'Wonderful,' said the school inspector.

'And I did all the illustrations,' said Araminta, boasting.

'Lovely,' said the school inspector, wishing that all children were as polite and well behaved.

When he looked up Becky was at his side. 'I've come to show you *my* story,' she said, grinning.

'Oh, it's you,' said Mr Scruple, pulling a face. 'Mary Poppins.'

When his beady green eyes rested on Becky's book, the school inspector gasped. He had never seen anything quite so bad in all his life. It looked as if a spider had climbed out of a bottle of ink and scuttled across the pages. The writing was so untidy and the pages were crumpled and covered in grubby marks.

'I have never seen a book like this before,' he murmured.

'Thank you very much,' said Becky.

'And is your story about the beautiful Princess Charisma and the handsome prince?' asked Mr Scruple, still in shock.

'Yes,' said Becky, 'but in mine a slimy green monster with sharp teeth and long claws climbs up the castle wall and swallows the beautiful Princess Charisma in one gulp. Then it chases after the handsome prince and gobbles him up on the little wooden bridge.'

'Oh,' was all the school inspector could bring himself to say.

'Look at *my* illustration,' said Becky,
waving a paint-splodged finger in
Mr Scruple's direction. In her picture,
which filled a whole page, the only part

of Princess Charisma that could be seen was her head, complete with little crown, popping out of the monster's mouth. 'She's screaming,' Becky told him. Then she stared for a moment at the stunned school inspector. 'Oops,' she said, 'I've got paint all over your jacket.'

At morning break Becky found the school inspector walking around the playground. She thought he looked lonely and felt a bit sorry for him. It would be all right to talk to him now. After all, he wasn't a stranger any more. She skipped up to him. 'Do you want to play conkers?' she asked.

'No, thank you,' Mr Scruple replied,

and headed for the school entrance.

Becky followed him. 'Why are oranges round?' she asked.

'I don't know,' he replied, quickening his pace.

'Why are holes empty?' asked Becky, skipping by his side.

'I don't know that either.'

'Why are bananas bent?'

'I don't know!' snapped Mr Scruple, speeding up.

'Why are your ears so red?' asked Becky.

'Why don't you go and ask somebody else,' he groaned, 'and leave me alone?' Becky skipped off to play conkers with Gareth, thinking to herself that school inspectors didn't seem to know very much.

Mr Scruple wiped his forehead and sighed. He had never met a child like Becky before and would be glad to be on his way.

At lunchtime, Becky found Mr Scruple in the dining room eating his lunch. When she sat down next to him he made a sort of funny strangled noise. It was the sort of noise her father made when Mr Whinger from next door came round to complain about her, or the noise that Miss Drear made when Becky interrupted her stories.

'I can talk to you now,' said Becky

brightly, 'because you're not a stranger any more.'

'I don't want you to talk to me,' said Mr Scruple, his small green eyes flashing. 'I want to be left alone.'

'I like baked beans,' said Becky, ignoring him and digging her fork into a huge mound on her plate. 'They're my favourite.'

'Really?' said the school inspector, scraping back his chair as he got ready to make his escape.

'Where are you going now?' asked Becky.

'I'm going to the school library,' Mr Scruple told her, 'and I don't want you to follow me.'

'It's over there,' Becky told him, waving her fork in front of him.

SPLAT! Mr Scruple received a faceful of baked beans. They dribbled down his sharp nose and dripped on to his tie, down his shirt and then on to his suit.

'Thank you,' he said, glaring at Becky. 'Thank you very much.'

Becky bit her lip and tried hard not to smile.

*

In the afternoon, the school inspector listened to the children reading. Araminta read her book about little lambs frisking in the meadow. Simon read his book about the helpful elf. Becky hated those sorts of stories. They were soppy. She liked a bit of action and adventure.

When Mr Scruple saw Becky heading towards him with her book under her arm he screwed up his face as if he were sucking a lemon. 'Oh no, not her,' he groaned to himself.

'I've come to read to you,' said Becky.

Mr Scruple didn't say a word but she noticed that he looked at her with a very sad and sorry expression.

'You've got a big stain down the front

of your jacket and on your tie and shirt,'
Becky informed him.

'Is that right?' Mr Scruple said
through gritted teeth.

'I like reading,' Becky told him.

'Really?'

'My story is about a man-eating shark
with big sharp teeth.'

'I thought it might be,' said Mr
Scruple.

'It gobbles people up,' said Becky.

'I guessed it would.'

'Shall I start?' asked Becky cheerfully.

'Go ahead,' the school inspector
sighed, rubbing his forehead as if he had
a really bad headache.

Becky read, putting in extra gruesome

details and making
blood-curdling
crunching
and slurping
noises as
the shark
gobbled
everyone up.

'Thank you,'
whispered the school inspector when she
had finished, his face as white as the
paper in the book.

'Shall I read you another about the
killer alien from outer space?' asked
Becky, feeling pleased with herself.

'No, no, thank you,' spluttered Mr
Scruple. 'That's more than enough.'

'I'm a good reader, aren't I?'

'Very good,' said Mr Scruple, glancing at his watch to see how much longer he would have to remain in the school and endure this impossible child.

'Is that your job,' asked Becky, 'going round schools listening to children read?'

'Yes, it is,' said Mr Scruple, staring at the dried orange stain on his tie and the paint stains on his jacket.

'And do you get paid for it?'

'Yes, I do.'

'Don't you have a proper job?'

Mr Scruple was now trembling. He looked quite ill.

Becky scratched her head, deep in thought.

'I think I'd like to be a school inspector when I grow up,' she said eventually, snapping her book shut like the mouth of a man-eating shark and making Mr Scruple jump. 'It seems to me to be a *really* easy job and you get to meet lots of nice people.'

Mr Scruple picked up his big black bag and headed for the classroom door without so much as a goodbye to Miss Drear. Becky smiled to herself and opened her favourite book about killer aliens.

Becky the Hero

There was a sharp rap on the front door.

'Whoever can that be, at this time?'
said Dad.

It was eight o'clock on a Saturday
morning and the family had just sat down
for breakfast.

'I'll go,' said Bernard, jumping up excitedly and heading for the door. 'It will be the postman. I'm expecting a letter from my penfriend in America.'

Becky dug her spoon into the mountain of cornflakes in front of her and crunched noisily. She had an idea who it might be but she carried on eating, hoping against hope it *would* be the postman. But it wasn't.

At the door stood the next-door neighbour, Mr Whinger, holding a bunch of broken stalks. There were no flowers on the end – they were just stalks. He was bright red in the face and breathing heavily. Becky hunched down in her chair, concentrating on her cereal.

'Is your mother or father in, Benjamin?' he asked Bernard angrily, getting the twins mixed up as usual.

Both Mum and Dad hurried to the door. 'Good morning, Mr Whinger,' they said together.

'It's not a good morning at all,' he told them, glowering. 'It's a bad morning, a very bad morning, that's what it is.' He held up the broken stalks and waved them in Mum and Dad's faces. 'Just look at these! My lovely flowers all ruined.'

'Oh dear,' said Mum.

'You had better come in,' said Dad, sighing deeply.

Mr Whinger strode into the kitchen. Becky slid down further in her chair. When Mr Whinger caught sight of her, he ballooned with anger. 'And that young lady,' he exclaimed, jiggling the broken stalks in front of him and going even redder in the face, 'is the reason it's a bad morning!'

'I didn't mean
to tread on
your flowers,
Mr Whinger,'
said Becky in
a very small and
sugary voice.

Becky was used to putting on her
angelic face and smiling her sweetest
smile. She could often win Mum and
Dad over like that. But it clearly wasn't
working with Mr Whinger, who
continued to screw up his bright-red face
as if he were wearing really tight shoes
that were pinching his toes.

'No, and I suppose you never meant
to climb over my fence and break it, or

push through my hedge and leave a big hole, or kick your ball into my garden and smash my greenhouse window, or let your rabbit wander into my vegetable patch and eat all my radishes.'

'Oh, Becky,' sighed Mum.

'Oh, Becky,' said Dad, shaking his head.

Becky never meant to cause any damage in Mr Whinger's garden. It just seemed to happen whenever she was out having fun.

'If I had a penny for every time I tell your Becky not to come into my garden,' said Mr Whinger, shaking the stalks, 'I'd be a millionaire by now.'

'We are very sorry, Mr Whinger,' said Mum.

'And we'll pay for any damage,' Dad added.

'Just keep her out of my garden!' cried Mr Whinger, marching out. Before anyone had a chance to draw breath he marched back in. 'And there's another thing.' He stabbed his finger in Becky's direction. 'When you pass my house on your way to school, young lady, stop peering in at my window. You're a nosy girl as well as a naughty one,' he said. 'Why can't you be more like your brothers?' And on that note Mr Whinger marched back out.

Becky took another massive mouthful of cornflakes and crunched noisily. She thought Mr Whinger was being very unfair.

For one thing, it was a rickety old fence anyway, and the hedge had lots of holes in it already and she didn't mean to kick her ball into Mr Whinger's soppy old garden and smash his greenhouse window. And it definitely wasn't her fault that Bumper, her pet rabbit, had wandered into his vegetable patch and eaten all his radishes. The trouble with Mr Whinger, Becky thought, was that he just liked complaining.

'When you have had your breakfast, Rebecca,' said Dad, 'I would like a serious word with you in the front room.'

'OK,' mumbled Becky, spitting out bits of milk and cornflakes.

Later, staring out of her bedroom window after the predicted telling-off from Dad and the warning never to go into Mr Whinger's garden again upon pain of being sent to her room *every* night with no television and a stop to her pocket money, Becky began to think about things. Mr Whinger, she decided, was one of those people who never smiled, was always mean and bad-tempered and was horrible to children. He would get on really well with her head teacher, Mrs Groucher. She wondered what he was like when he was a little boy. *I bet he told tales*, she thought, *never shared his sweets and was probably cross all the time and absolutely no fun whatsoever.*

Anyway, Becky thought grumpily, Mr Whinger and her dad were both wrong. It really wasn't her fault. It was her rabbit that was the cause of all the trouble.

Bumper was a huge, flop-eared, pale-brown creature with long white whiskers and great round eyes. Every morning, before school, Becky took Bumper out of his hutch for his exercise. There wasn't much of interest in Becky's garden for a lively, hungry rabbit in search of adventure but there was next door.

Mr Whinger's garden was not like Becky's. Her garden had the remains of a lawn, a large dead tree with a hole in the trunk, overgrown borders full of tall weeds and nettles, and an old garden shed that Becky used as a den. There were no flowers or bushes. It used to be quite neat and tidy until Becky was old enough to start trampling through the flowerbeds and then Dad had stopped bothering with gardening. Anyway, Becky liked it just as it was.

Mr Whinger's garden, separated from hers by a high wooden fence (part of which was broken) and a thick hedge (with holes in it), was very different. There was a long green lawn, borders full of colourful flowers, a neat vegetable plot, a little greenhouse (with a broken window) and a pond full of fat orange fish.

Bumper liked to hop though the hedge into Mr Whinger's garden or burrow under the fence and nibble his way to the vegetable patch. This is exactly what Bumper had been up to yesterday.

Becky had tried to stop him but he was too quick for her and had soon found his way into Mr Whinger's garden. She had pushed through the hole in the hedge after him and that's when the flowers had been trampled on.

Honestly! thought Becky. Why Mr Whinger and her dad couldn't see that Bumper was to blame for all the damage was a mystery to her.

*

The following Sunday, Becky was heading for the rabbit hutch when Mr Whinger's face appeared over the fence.

'I'm going out,' he told Becky, 'and you stay out of my garden, young lady, or else.'

'Huh,' mumbled Becky when his head had disappeared, 'he's as grumpy and bad-tempered as ever. I hope he's gone all day.'

Becky took her rabbit out of his hutch and put him gently on the scrubby lawn.

'Now, you be good,' she told him sternly. Bumper hopped about a bit, nibbled a tuft of dry grass, investigated the overgrown borders and then his nose started to twitch. He had got a whiff of the radishes next door and off he hopped in the direction of Mr Whinger's garden.

'No!' cried Becky, as the rabbit took a leap towards the hedge. 'You'll get me into terrible trouble again if you go into Mr Whinger's garden.'

As usual, Bumper took no notice. Rabbits can't understand little girls, but they can smell fat juicy red radishes ripe for nibbling. In a trice he had burrowed through to the next-door neighbour's garden.

It was a good thing, Becky thought to herself as she pushed her way through the hole in the fence, that Mr Whinger had gone out. She tiptoed carefully around the flowers and found Bumper in the middle of a big patch of radishes, munching away.

'Come here, you naughty rabbit,' said Becky, gently picking him up and cradling him in her arms.

It was then that she noticed the man on the small balcony outside Mr Whinger's bedroom window. There was a ladder leaning up against the wall.

Becky knew she wasn't supposed to talk to strangers but when she saw big footprints in the borders and some plant pots that had been knocked over, she decided there was no way that she going to take the blame.

'What are you doing?' shouted Becky. The man was so startled that he nearly fell off the balcony. 'Oh, you made me jump!' he cried.

'What are you doing?' Becky repeated.

'I'm cleaning the windows,' the man told her cheerfully.

'But Mr Whinger always cleans his own windows,' said Becky. 'I've seen him.'

'Well, I'm doing them!' snapped the man.

'Mr Whinger cleaned his windows yesterday,' said Becky. 'I saw him.'

'Well, he's asked me to do it again today,' growled the man. He stared at Becky menacingly.

She did not like the look of this man at all. With his small eyes, pointed nose, gleaming white teeth and glossy black hair bristling on his head, he looked just like the rat that Becky had seen in the pet shop. She thought it best not to get any closer to his ladder.

'Why don't you go and play with your dolls? There's a good little girl,' said the man.

'I haven't got any dolls,' Becky told him. She liked this man less and less by the minute. 'Where's your bucket?'

'What?' snapped the man.

'Window cleaners have buckets and cloths. Where are yours?'

'They're round the front,' said the man, looking angry.

'Why?'

'What?'

'Why are they round the front if you're cleaning windows round the back?' Becky persisted.

'You ask too many questions, little girl,' said the man, smiling.

It wasn't a very nice smile, Becky thought.

'My dad says that if you don't know, you should ask,' Becky informed him. 'So, why *is* your bucket round the front?'

'Why don't you go home, little girl, and mind your own business?' said the man, losing his patience.

'I don't think you're a window cleaner at all,' said Becky. 'I think you're a burglar.'

'No, no,' said the man, laughing. 'I'm a friend of Mr Roper.'

'His name's Mr Whinger,' said Becky.

The man frowned. 'I'm coming down,' he said, moving towards the ladder.

'Oh no, you're not!' said Becky and, putting Bumper on the ground, she ran

towards the ladder and pushed it
with all her strength.

It slid across the wall and clattered noisily on to the path.

'Why did you do that, you horrible little girl?' shouted the man. 'Now I can't get down.'

'Then you'll have to wait until Mr Whinger comes home,' said Becky triumphantly.

At that very moment, Mr Whinger came round the corner of the house. When he saw Becky in his garden holding her rabbit, he ballooned with anger. 'You . . . you . . . What did I say about coming into my garden?' he shouted. He looked as if he were about to explode. 'You're a very disobedient, naughty girl!'

Becky put Bumper down, folded her
arms across her chest and waited
patiently until Mr Whinger had stopped
shouting and jumping
up and down.

'I saw this man on your balcony,' said
Becky eventually. 'He said he was
cleaning your windows.'

'What man?' spluttered Mr Whinger.
Becky pointed up to the balcony. 'That
man, up there,' she said. 'I think he's a
burglar.' And with that, Becky picked up
Bumper and pushed her way back
through the hedge and into her own
garden.

Later that day there was a sharp rap on
the front door.

'Whoever can that be?' said Dad.
This time it was six o'clock and the
family was sitting down having their
dinner. Becky had just pushed a big

spoonful of pudding into her mouth. She
had an idea who it might be.

'I'll go,' said Bernard, jumping up and
heading for the door.

Ben ran to
the window
and peered
out. 'It's a
policeman!'
he cried.
'And there's
Mr Whinger
with him
and I think
he's holding
some broken
plants.'

'Oh dear,' sighed Mum.

Becky dug her spoon into the bowlful of pudding and chomped noisily.

Bernard opened the door.

'Good afternoon, young man,' said the policeman. 'I'm Police Constable Catchum. Are your parents in?'

'Yes,' said Bernard.

Dad went to the door with a tragic expression on his face. He prepared himself for the worst. 'You had better come in,' he sighed.

Police Constable Catchum and Mr Whinger followed Dad into the kitchen.

'It's about your daughter,' Constable Catchum informed Becky's parents in a serious tone of voice.

'I thought it might be,' murmured Dad. 'Whatever has she done now?'

Becky continued to eat her pudding and stared innocently at her family. Everyone looked so serious.

'You should be very proud of that young lady,' the police constable continued.

'What?' exclaimed Becky's mum.

'Proud?' gasped Dad.

The twins just sat there looking amazed.

Becky wiped the custard from her mouth and beamed.

'If it hadn't been for her quick thinking,' said the policeman, patting Becky on the head, 'Fred Filcher, the burglar, would have broken in and stolen all of Mr Whinger's valuables. Now, as I always tell children, it is not a sensible thing to approach strangers or to talk to them, but –'

'He was on the balcony,' said Becky. 'He was miles away and if I had gone to fetch Dad he would have got away. Anyway, I had Bumper with me and he's got a really nasty bite.'

'And speaking of that rabbit,' said Mr Whinger, holding up a big bunch of bright-red radishes, 'I thought Bumper might enjoy these.'

'Thanks,' said Becky, spitting out bits of custard and pudding, and smiling fit to burst. 'I think he might.'